D0952109

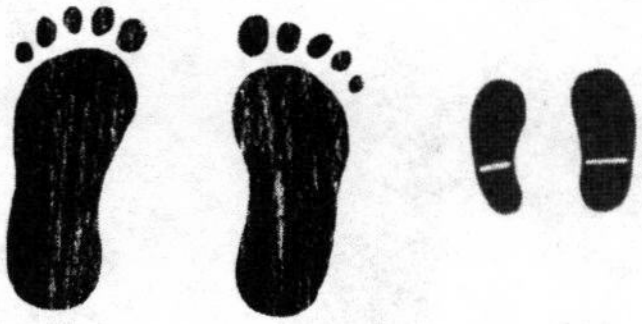

BIG FOOT
and LITTLE FOOT

BOOK 2

THE MONSTER DETECTOR

Story by Ellen Potter
Art by Felicita Sala

AMULET BOOKS

NEW YORK

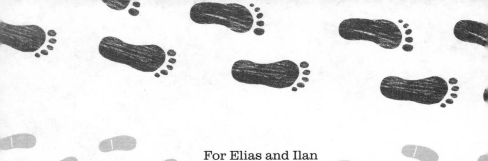

For Elias and Ilan

PUBLISHER'S NOTE: This is a work
of fiction. Names, characters, places,
and incidents are either the product of the
author's imagination or used fictitiously, and any
resemblance to actual persons, living or dead, business
establishments, events, or locales is entirely coincidental.

Library of Congress Cataloging-in-Publication Data

Names: Potter, Ellen, 1963- author. | Sala, Felicita, illustrator.
Title: The Monster Detector / by Ellen Potter; illustrated by Felicita Sala.
Description: New York: Amulet Books, 2018. | Series: Big foot and little foot; Book 2
| Summary: Hugo, a young sasquatch, and his friend Gigi use a Monster Detector to find
a Green Whistler, but when Hugo's human friend, Boone, joins in, surprises are in store.
Identifiers: LCCN 2018001832 | ISBN 978-1-4197-3122-8 (hardcover pob)
Subjects: | CYAC: Yeti—Fiction. | Monsters—Fiction. | Schools—Fiction. | Friendship—
Fiction.
Classification: LCC PZ7.P8518 Mo 2018 | DDC [E]—dc23

Text copyright © 2018 Ellen Potter
Illustrations copyright © 2018 Felicita Sala
Book design by Siobhán Gallagher

Published in 2018 by Amulet Books, an imprint of ABRAMS. All rights reserved. No
portion of this book may be reproduced, stored in a retrieval system, or transmitted
in any form or by any means, mechanical, electronic, photocopying, recording, or
otherwise, without written permission from the publisher.

Amulet Books® is a registered trademark of Harry N. Abrams, Inc.

Printed and bound in U.S.A.
10 9 8 7 6 5 4 3 2 1

Amulet Books are available at special discounts when purchased in quantity
for premiums and promotions as well as fundraising or educational use.
Special editions can also be created to specification. For details, contact
specialsales@abramsbooks.com or the address below.

ABRAMS The Art of Books
195 Broadway, New York, NY 10007
abramsbooks.com

The Big Foot and Little Foot series

Book One: *Big Foot and Little Foot*

Book Two: *The Monster Detector*

Book Three: *The Squatchicorns*

1

Monster in a Box

Deep in the cold North Woods, there lived a young Sasquatch named Hugo. He was bigger than you but smaller than me, and he was hairier than both of us. He lived in apartment 1G in the very back of Widdershins Cavern with his mother and father and his older sister, Winnie.

It was Saturday, which was the day that mail was delivered to Widdershins Cavern. Hugo stood at the end of the long line at the post office, waiting to see if his package had arrived. Every so often he would jump up as high as he could.

"What are you doing, Hugo?" asked a voice behind him. It was his friend Gigi. She was on the small side for a squidge (which is what you call a young Sasquatch) but she had excellent posture, which made her look a little taller. She was holding a letter.

"I'm waiting in line," he answered.

"No, I mean, why are you jumping up and down?" Gigi asked.

"I'm trying to see if there's a large package on the post office shelf," Hugo replied.

"If there is, it might be mine." He jumped up again, but he couldn't see over the heads of all the grown-up Sasquatches in front of him.

"What's in the package?" Gigi asked.

"I'm not sure," he answered. "It's from Mad Marvin."

"Mad Marvin? You mean the guy who makes Mad Marvin's Monster Cards?"

Hugo nodded. "If you collect one hundred wrappers from Mad Marvin's Monster Cards and mail them in, Mad Marvin will send you a special prize. I mailed mine in last week. I've been collecting them for three years. No one in all of Widdershins Cavern has ever collected that many wrappers."

Gigi crossed her arms over her chest and stared hard at Hugo. "You think Mad Marvin is sending you a monster, don't you, Hugo?"

"No," Hugo answered quickly. But after a moment, he admitted, "Well, maybe." Suddenly he had an idea. "Hey, Gigi, if you climb up on my shoulders, you'll be able to see if there's a large package on the shelf." Then he remembered that Gigi was sensitive about being small, so he added, "I mean, I *would* climb on *your* shoulders, but you have better balance than I do."

Gigi thought about this for a second. A special prize was always interesting, even if it wasn't a monster.

"Okay," she said. "Hold this." She handed her letter to Hugo.

He knelt down and Gigi climbed onto his shoulders. Slowly, he stood up while she gripped the long hair on his neck.

"Do you see anything?" he asked after a moment.

"I see Mrs. Rattlebags," Gigi said. "She's

at the counter, complaining about some-thing."

"That's nothing new," said Hugo. Mrs. Rattlebags was always complaining about something.

"But do you see a package?" he asked impatiently.

"Yep," said Gigi. "And it's so big they couldn't even put it on the shelf. They put it on the floor instead."

"How big is it?" Hugo asked excitedly.

Gigi considered. "You could fit a squidge in it," she said.

A squidge . . . *or a monster*, thought Hugo.

"And it's in a wooden crate," Gigi contin-ued. "Wait, there are words written on the

crate. The first word is . . . CAUTION!"

CAUTION! That was a good sign, thought Hugo. If you were going to mail a monster, you would definitely write CAUTION! on the crate.

"What else does it say?" Hugo asked.

Gigi wiggled around on his shoulders, then said, "I can't see. Can you stand on your tiptoes?"

Hugo stood on his tiptoes.

"Higher," she said.

He stood on the very tip of his tiptoes.

"It says LIVE CARGO!," Gigi told him.

"LIVE CARGO! Then there is a monster in

there!" he cried. Hugo got so excited that he forgot to keep still. Gigi bobbled around on his shoulders, then slid down his back in a very undignified way. She fell on the ground, backside first.

"Sorry," Hugo said as he helped her to her feet.

After *harrumphing* with annoyance, Gigi patted down the three thin braids on the side of her head and stood up even straighter than before.

"I told you!" Hugo said. "Mad Marvin *did* send a monster! I wonder which one it is. It could be a Shivering Wisp. Or a Black-Toed Oozer . . . no, that's bigger than two squidges. Maybe it's a Six-Headed Screecher."

"Hugo, monsters aren't real," Gigi said.

"Of course they're real. For instance, I always thought Humans were a kind of monster, until I met Boone." Boone was Hugo's best friend, a Human boy who lived on the banks of Ripple Worm River. "And Boone thought Sasquatches were monsters until he met us. A monster is just a creature you've never seen before and are a little afraid of. But when you meet it, it's just sort of . . . regular. But better."

Gigi thought about that for a second. She was an excellent thinker, and in the end she had to admit that made perfect sense.

2

Mad Marvin's Special Prize

As the line inched forward, Hugo could hardly stand the suspense. He wondered what his mother would say about the monster. If it was a Shivering Wisp, she might think it was cute. Still, Hugo would prefer a Six-Headed Screecher. He wondered if you had to feed all six of the heads.

Hugo couldn't wait to show the monster to Boone. Boone knew all about monsters. He and Hugo were going to become cryptozoologists when they grew up. (A cryptozoologist is a hard-to-say word for someone who studies mysterious creatures.) Now Hugo and Boone would have a real, live monster to take care of!

Finally, Hugo and Gigi reached the post office counter.

"Hi, Mr. Kipper!" Hugo said to the postmaster as he bounced up and down with anticipation.

"Well, good morning, Hugo. You look like someone who is expecting a package today."

Hugo nodded and looked at the crate on the floor.

"Well, I might just have something with your name on it." Mr. Kipper winked. Then he turned around, but instead of lifting up the crate, he went to the shelf and picked up a little square package.

"Here you go." Mr. Kipper handed Hugo the little package. Hugo's name and address were written on it, and Mad Marvin's name was written above the return address. The package was so small it fit in the palm of Hugo's hand. It did not say WARNING or LIVE CARGO on the package. Instead, it said FRAGILE.

That meant whatever was inside it could be broken.

And since monsters cannot be broken, it also meant that there was no monster inside.

"Is there anything else for me?" Hugo asked Mr. Kipper in a small but hopeful voice, still eyeballing the large crate.

"No, I'm afraid that's it."

"Oh. Well . . . thanks," Hugo said.

Hugo waited while Gigi mailed her letter, and the two of them walked out of the post office.

"Well? Aren't you going to open your package?" Gigi asked him.

Hugo shrugged. "I guess so."

It was hard to get excited about something that wasn't a monster.

Hugo tore open the package, pulled out a little wooden box, and removed the lid. Both he and Gigi stared down at what was inside.

"Hmm," said Gigi.

"Hmm," said Hugo.

It was a little square piece of wood. In the middle of the square was a round glass window with five white specks inside.

"What do you think it is?" Hugo asked.

"It looks like a compass. Sort of."

Hugo took it out of its box. There was a black strap attached to it.

"It's not a compass, it's a watch!" said Hugo excitedly. He'd never owned a watch before.

"I don't think it's a watch, either," said Gigi. "Wait. There's a note in the box."

She pulled out the note and unfolded it. This is what it said:

Congratulations! You are now the proud owner of a genuine Monster Detector! Inside your detector are five weechie-weechie moths. When a monster is nearby, they will make a clicking sound by flapping their wings.

We have included a bag of weechie-weechie food. Open the lid on the back of the detector and drop in a pinch each week, along with a drop of water.

Here are a few of the monsters you might find with your Monster Detector:

Red-Nosed Gruzzles, Thorny Wrigglers, Pink-Eyed Pookas, and Hairless Wolly-Wollys.

Good luck finding monsters!

Sincerely,

Mad Marvin

"Wow!" Hugo said, examining the Monster Detector.

"What's a Hairless Wolly-Wolly?" Gigi asked.

It wasn't often that Gigi asked Hugo a question. Gigi usually knew everything about everything. But Hugo did know more about monsters than she did.

"Let's see, a Hairless Wolly-Wolly . . ."

 Hugo looked up at the cavern's ceiling, then down at his hairy feet, and then back at Gigi. "It's about the size of a raccoon . . . and it has a scrunched-up

kind of face with long, pointy ears . . . and . . . it has no hair."

He wasn't absolutely sure about this, except for the "no hair" part.

"Oh." Gigi nodded. "Sounds weird."

"Well, it *is* a monster, after all."

"Until you meet it," Gigi said. "Then it's sort of regular."

"Regular . . . but better," Hugo reminded her.

3

The Monster Search

You know what we should do now?" Hugo said, strapping the Monster Detector on his wrist.

"Look for monsters?" Gigi guessed.

Hugo nodded.

"But how are we going to look for monsters if we can't go outside?" Gigi asked.

Squidges were only allowed to go outside the cavern once in a while, with their school and on special holidays. Although the Big Wide World was an exciting place, it was also dangerous for Sasquatches. There were all sorts of stories about Humans who hunted Sasquatches. Sometimes the Humans wanted to capture them and put them in a cage to study them. Sasquatches needed practice and skill to stay safe in the Big Wide World.

"We can look for monsters right here, in the cavern," suggested Hugo. "There might be one or two."

Gigi gave him a doubtful look.

"Maybe really small ones," he said.

They started their monster search by

traveling down to the east end of the cavern. But it was all apartments down on that end, with lots of Sasquatches going to and fro. It didn't seem like the sort of place a monster would be.

They turned around and headed to the west end of the cavern instead. It was quieter there. There were no apartments and no Sasquatches. They ambled along slowly while Hugo held out his wrist with the Monster Detector on it, and they listened for a *click-click* sound.

The cavern looked different here. The path was narrower. The rock walls were lumpy and had rusty orange lines swirling through them. Hugo and Gigi walked and walked, but the Monster Detector had not made a single sound.

"Maybe it's broken," said Hugo, stopping to tap on the detector's glass window.

"Or maybe there just aren't any monsters around here," Gigi said.

Click-click.

"Did you hear that?" Hugo whispered.

Gigi nodded.

Click-click. Click-click.

They looked at the Monster Detector. In the little glass window, the weechie-weechie moths were flapping their tiny wings.

Click-click! Click-click!

"There must be a monster here!" Hugo whispered.

They checked all around them, but they didn't see anything suspicious.

"Wait, look at that," Gigi said suddenly, pointing up.

There was an opening at the top of the wall where a thin sliver of light peeped through. Hugo held the Monster Detector up toward it.

CLICK-CLICK-CLICK-CLICK-CLICK!!!! went the weechie-weechie moths.

"The monster must be on the other side of the wall," whispered Gigi.

They both looked up at the opening at the top of the wall. It was high above the ground.

"I could climb up there and have a look," Hugo said.

He was pretty sure Gigi would tell him that that was a stupid idea. She would tell him that it was too dangerous.

But instead Gigi said, "It's the only way to find out."

"Right," he said.

He didn't move.

"I can't think of any other way," he said.

He still didn't move.

"Can you?" he asked.

"I'll do it if you don't want to," Gigi offered.

So of course Hugo had to say that he *did* want to.

He took a deep breath. Carefully, he placed his foot in a little hollow in the wall. He found a shallow ledge on which to place his hand. Slowly, he began to climb. His foot slipped once and he scrambled to find another ledge.

"Are you all right?" Gigi called up.

"I'm totally fine," he said.

Which was not really true. He was barely even mostly fine.

The higher he climbed, the more frantically the weechie-weechie moths *click-clicked.*

"*Shhh!*" he whispered to them.

Finally, Hugo gripped the edge of the hole in the wall. With all his strength, he pulled himself up and peered through the gap. His eyes grew wide. His mouth fell open.

"What?! What do you see?" Gigi whispered.

"Whoa!" was all Hugo could manage to say.

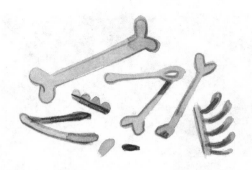

4

The Green Whistler

On the other side of the wall was a small room, no bigger than your bedroom closet. One of the walls in the room had an opening that led out to the Big Wide World. It was large enough for a full-grown Sasquatch to walk through, if they ducked their head a little. Scattered on the ground in the room were

clumps of dark green fur. In one corner there was a pile of small bones.

"Something lives here, Gigi," Hugo whispered down to her.

"A Sasquatch?" Gigi whispered back.

Hugo shook his head. "There are bones. Sasquatches don't eat meat."

"Maybe a bear?" Gigi suggested.

"Have you ever heard of a bear with green fur?" Hugo asked.

"Green fur?" Suddenly Gigi looked alarmed. "It must be the Green Whistler!"

Hugo felt his foot begin to slip, and he came back down to the ground in a sliding, skidding, bumping way.

"The Green Whatsit?" he asked as he checked his feet for scrapes.

"The Green *Whistler*! My grandmother told me about it. It was this horrible creature that used to live in Widdershins Cavern. They called it the Green Whistler because it was covered in green fur, and right before it pounced on its victims it made this weird whistling noise."

"Really?"

"Reálly. And my grandmother said there was a rumor that it ate squidges."

Hugo and Gigi stared at each other in the darkness. The only sound was the *click-click-click* of the Monster Detector.

"Um, I'd better get going," said Hugo. "I think my parents wanted me to help at the store."

"Yeah, I think I still have some homework to do," Gigi said.

Then Hugo and Gigi turned around and walked back the way they had come. But this time they walked *a lot* faster.

5

Snarfles

Hugo's family owned the Every-thing-You-Need General Store and Bakery. On Saturday morning the store was always busy. Today, all the little round tables were filled with customers eating blackberry snarfles, which are sort of like waffles except they are shaped like oak leaves.

Other customers were examining items on the store's shelves, like jugs of shampoo (most Sasquatches go through a dozen jugs of shampoo a month), and hacksaws and jigsaws and crosscut saws, because all Sasquatches are experts when it comes to making things out of wood. There were also colorful scarves for fashionable Sasquatches and diapers for baby Sasquatches, and high up on a shelf was a Human Repellent, which smelled just like skunk when you sprayed it. That

was for when you were walking in the woods and wanted Humans to stay away.

Hugo's mom was behind the counter, ringing up purchases. When she saw Hugo, she smiled and waved.

"Hugo!" she called to him over the customers' heads. "Can you run back to the kitchen and ask Grandpa to make some more mushroom tarts? We're all out!"

"Sure, Mom!" Hugo called back.

He started toward the kitchen, passing the little dining room where his sister,

Winnie, was working. She was wiping down a table with a wet rag very slowly while talking to two big Sasquatch boys sitting at the next table. Her lips were an alarming shade of purple and very shiny. She had slathered them with the huckleberry lip gloss that she made herself.

She stopped talking to the boys long enough to notice Hugo.

"What is that ridiculous thing on your wrist?" she asked him.

"It's a Monster Detector," Hugo replied.

"A Monster Detector!? *HA!*" Winnie blurted out, and the big Sasquatch boys looked at each other and smirked.

"*HA*, yourself! It actually works," Hugo

told her. "The bugs inside of it flap their wings and make a clicking sound whenever a monster is close by."

Winnie snorted. "Good thing it's not a Weirdo Detector or it would click whenever *you* got near it."

The Sasquatch boys laughed at that, and Winnie smiled at them.

Hugo held his wrist out toward Winnie and waved it around her head for a moment. "Well, I guess we know it's not a Big Flirt Detector," he said. "If it was, the bugs would be flapping so hard right now that their wings would fall off!"

Winnie's face turned a deep pink. She raised her arm with the dirty rag in it and chucked it at Hugo's head. He ducked just

in time, then made a quick dash for the kitchen.

Grandpa was pouring batter into the snarfle iron. The counter was lined with plates, waiting for more snarfles to be piled on top of them.

"Hi, Grandpa," Hugo said. "Mom says we need more mushroom tarts."

"More? But I made a dozen this morning! Phew, it's been busy today! Why don't you handle the snarfle iron while I make more tarts?"

"Sure!"

Hugo loved using the snarfle iron. He could make a perfect leaf-shaped snarfle almost as well as Grandpa.

Grandpa fired up the oven and opened the kitchen's back door so that the room wouldn't get too hot and smoky. Baking in a cavern could be tricky.

While Grandpa sliced mushrooms for the tarts, Hugo poured snarfle batter onto the hot snarfle iron.

"Grandpa," Hugo said, "do you know anything about the Green Whistler?"

Grandpa looked startled. "The Green Whistler! Well, well, well. I haven't heard that name since I was a little squidge. Why do you ask?"

"Because I think I saw it. Or at least, I

saw where it lives." Hugo described how he and Gigi found the little room at the west end of the cavern and how he had climbed to the top of the wall to peek in. "There were bones and green fur and everything."

Grandpa frowned. "You and Gigi shouldn't have been wandering around the cavern like that, Hugo."

"I know. But Grandpa, did the Green Whistler really eat squidges?"

There was no answer. Grandpa seemed deep in thought. Hugo repeated his question.

"Oh, no, no," Grandpa answered, "that was just a lot of silly talk."

But there was no doubt about it . . . Grandpa looked worried.

6

The Academy for Curious Squidges

Before school started on Monday, all the squidges gathered around Hugo to look at his Monster Detector.

"Doth ip erk?" asked Izzy.

Izzy wore headgear for his overbite, so he spoke a little funny. Fortunately, Hugo almost always understood him.

"Of course it works!" Hugo said. "In

fact, it's already found a monster." He told them about the Green Whistler, and when they didn't believe him, Gigi said it was all true, every word of it.

Just then, Mrs. Nukluk entered the classroom. They all rushed over to their desks and sat down. As usual, Mrs. Nukluk was wearing her long white cloak made of goose feathers.

"Good morning, class," she said. "We've got a busy day ahead of us, and later this morning I have a big surprise for you!"

The squidges looked at each other excitedly.

"Maybe it's a microscope," Gigi whispered to Hugo.

Hugo hoped it was something more fun than a microscope, but he didn't say that to Gigi.

"Does the surprise explode?" asked Malcolm.

"No, it does not, and please raise your hand if you have something to say."

Malcolm raised his hand. "Are you going to pull an egg out of your nose?"

"Why on *earth* would I do that, Malcolm?"

"Because you said there was going to be a big surprise. And that would be very surprising."

Mrs. Nukluk took a deep breath. Deep

breaths seemed to help her when she spoke to Malcolm.

"Take out your math books, everyone. We'll start right in on measurements—"

At that moment a small Human boy walked into the classroom. He had thirty-eight freckles and he carried a paper bag.

"Boone!" cried Hugo.

You weren't supposed to shout in class, but Hugo was so shocked to see his friend that he couldn't help himself.

"Is Boone the surprise, Mrs. Nukluk?" asked Pip.

"No," said Mrs. Nukluk, "but I must admit I *am* surprised. What are you doing here, Boone?"

"I've been thinking about it, and I've

finally decided—" said Boone, smiling at them all. "I want to go to squidge school!"

7

Snuds and Stonkers

Mrs. Nukluk looked confused. "Don't you have your own school? A *Human* school?" she asked.

"I'm homeschooled. But my grandmother said that if a school opened up in the North Woods, I could go to it. And now that I know about the Academy for

Curious Squidges, I've decided I want to go."

"Well . . . well . . . we've never had a Human in our school. I'm not sure if it's . . ." Mrs. Nukluk searched for the right word.

"Please, Mrs. Nukluk, *please* let Boone join our school!" cried Hugo.

Mrs. Nukluk was so flustered that she forgot to remind Hugo to raise his hand.

"I know all my state capitals," Boone said to her. "And I can spell pretty good, except I get my *f*'s and *ph*'s mixed up sometimes. Plus, I brought my own lunch." He held up his bag.

Mrs. Nukluk considered. "Well, I suppose you can spend the day here. After that, we'll just have to see. There's an empty seat next to Roderick. You can sit there for now."

Roderick Rattlebags's hand shot up in the air.

"Yes, Roderick?"

"I refuse to sit next to a Human," Roderick said in a puffed-up way.

Boone had been walking happily over to Roderick's desk, but now he stopped short. His smile disappeared.

"Boone is just as good as any squidge!" Gigi snapped at Roderick.

"And better than some!" Hugo added, glaring at Roderick.

"Our school is called the Academy for Curious *Squidges*," Roderick shot back at them in a spiteful way, "not Curious *Humans*."

"That's enough," Mrs. Nukluk said. "Please sit down, Boone." Then she turned a stern face to Roderick. "You will share your math book with Boone."

Roderick made a disgusted huffing noise while Boone sat down next to him. The desk and chair were made for squidges, who are much larger than Human children. Boone's head barely peeped over the desk, and his legs dangled off the ground. Roderick looked down at him with a sneer and shifted his chair as far away from Boone as possible.

Mrs. Nukluk led the class through a review of what they had been learning the past week in math. It was all easy stuff, like how many shucklings were in a snud.

Boone raised his hand.

"Yes, Boone?" said Mrs. Nukluk.

"What's a snud?" he asked.

The whole class turned to stare at him, flabbergasted. Even the smallest squidges knew what a snud was!

"It's a unit of measurement," said Mrs. Nukluk. "It's about half the size of a stonker."

"A what?" asked Boone.

Hugo frowned. What was Boone's grandmother teaching him if he didn't even know what a snud or a stonker were?

Mrs. Nukluk opened up her desk drawer and took out her measuring stick. It was a straight piece of maple branch with marks burned into it.

"You see, Boone," she said patiently, placing one finger about halfway up the stick, "this much is a snud."

Boone squinted at the stick

for a moment. Then he smiled his big smile. "*Ohhh!* I get it! A snud is a foot!"

"Excuse me?" Mrs. Nukluk looked confused.

"A snud is a foot," Boone repeated.

"A snud is a *snud*," Mrs. Nukluk said firmly.

"Which is also a foot," insisted Boone.

Now, you and I both know that Boone meant a "foot" in the measuring sort of way, such as "there are twelve inches in a foot." But Sasquatches don't know about feet and yards and inches. That's why Mrs. Nukluk's face suddenly grew very irritated.

"A snud is *not* a foot," she told Boone sternly. "It's not a hand nor an earlobe nor a tongue either. And if you are going to be in this classroom, you'll have to behave and not act so silly."

Boone turned bright red. He slumped in his seat while Roderick smirked at him.

Things had not gotten off to a good start.

8

X-treme Creepy Cryptids

After math, everyone carved little owls out of stumps in woodshop. I know that sounds like fun—and it is—but for Sasquatches, woodworking is very serious business. Sasquatches make nearly everything out of wood, so even the littlest squidges have to learn to do it well.

Luckily, Boone had already done lots of wood carving. Before long he had carved an owl that was just as nice as any of the squidges', and Mrs. Nukluk said so, too.

After woodworking came recess. Everyone bolted out of their chairs to play the Ha-Ha Game or Frog King, which involves a lot of hopping and clapping and kicking, and someone almost always winds up getting hurt, but only just a little.

Hugo hurried over to Boone, who was sliding off his squidge-sized chair.

"I brought something to show you," Boone said, reaching into his back pocket. He pulled out a thick stack of cards with a rubber band around them. The cards had colorful pictures of strange creatures on them.

"What is that?" Hugo asked as he eagerly watched Boone take off the rubber band.

"They're called X-treme Creepy Cryptids cards," Boone told him.

Izzy and Malcolm, who were playing Frog King nearby, overheard and ran over to look.

"What are cryptids?" asked Malcolm.

"Well, they're sort of like monsters," said Boone.

"Wow! So these are Monster Cards for *Humans*!" Malcolm said this so loud that it brought the rest of the class over, too. Even Roderick sauntered over, peering at the cards while pretending not to be interested.

Boone gave each squidge a small stack to look at. On one side there was a colorful picture of a cryptid, and on the other side there was information about it. The monsters on the X-treme Creepy Cryptids cards were different from the monsters on Mad Marvin's cards. On Boone's cards there was a chupacabra, and the Jersey Devil, and a Goatman, which had a Human body and the head of a goat with horns. There were mermaids and mermen, and a sewer alligator. There was even a card for an Ogopogo, a creature that Hugo and Boone had once spotted on the Ripple Worm River.

Hugo was so happy that Boone was making friends, he had to bite his lip to keep from smiling the whole time.

The squidges read all about the cryptids on the backs of the cards. But Boone also told them extra things about the cryptids that weren't even on the cards.

"How do you know all this stuff?" Malcolm asked Boone.

"Because I'm going to be a cryptozoologist one day," Boone told him. "So is Hugo. We have to know all about cryptids."

"Why? So you can capture them?" asked Malcolm.

"No, so we can *understand* them. A cryptozoologist is sort of like a cryptid's best friend."

"*Eww*, look at this thing!" said Pip, holding up a card showing a huge, creepy-looking beast. Its mouth was open as though it were roaring, showing long, sharp fangs dripping with gooey saliva. Its angry eyes were red and squinty. It was covered with tangled hair, and it held up a club as though it were about to thwack it down on someone's head.

"Can I see that?" asked Gigi. Pip handed her the card, and Gigi read from the back:

SASQUATCH

Also known as Bigfoot.
Stinks like a skunk. Not
very intelligent. Can't speak
but makes grunting noises.
Might eat people. Found in
forests and mountainous
areas all over the world.

Everyone was silent. They were all
shocked, even Hugo.

"But we don't eat people," Pip said finally,
in a hurt voice. "We don't eat meat at all."

"Unlike Humans," Roderick grumbled. "Humans will eat just about anything."

"And we don't make grunting noises," said Malcolm.

"Of course not!" said Boone quickly. "These are just dumb old cards."

"Do Humans really think we're monsters?" Pip asked Boone.

"I guess some Humans do—" Boone started to say.

"Well, that's just . . . that's just . . . awful!" Pip said angrily, and she shoved her stack of cards back at Boone and stomped off.

"I dek bads eber day," said Izzy before handing back his cards and walking away.

"What did he say?" asked Boone.

"He said, 'I take baths every day,'" Hugo translated.

The other squidges left, too. Even Gigi quietly slipped away.

"Wait, guys . . . *I* don't think Sasquatches are monsters!" Boone called out to them, but everyone pretended not to hear him.

Hugo put his arm around Boone's shoulder.

"Don't worry, Boone. They'll get used to you. Remember, this is the first day a Human has ever gone to our school."

And I hope it's not the last day, too, Hugo couldn't help thinking.

9

Mrs. Nukluk's Big Surprise

After recess, Mrs. Nukluk said that it was time for the big surprise. She stepped out of the room to go get it. Pip made a squeak of excitement, while Izzy bounced in his chair. Even Hugo had forgotten to be upset about Boone and was now staring at the door, eagerly waiting for Mrs. Nukluk's surprise.

"I bet it's a trampoline," said Malcolm.

"Shhh!" Gigi said. "If she catches us talking she won't give us the surprise at all."

They heard Mrs. Nukluk's thumping footsteps coming back down the hall. Everyone sat up straight in their chairs.

After a minute Mrs. Nukluk walked into the classroom carrying a very large wooden crate. On the front of the crate, it said CAUTION! LIVE CARGO!

"It's the crate from the post office!" Hugo cried, before he could stop himself.

"*Shhhh!*" all the squidges told him.

Mrs. Nukluk placed the crate on the floor. She smoothed down the goose feathers on her cloak, then looked at all of them and smiled.

"Is everyone ready for the surprise?" she asked.

"*YEEESSSS!*" they all shouted.

Mrs. Nukluk squinched up her eyes and stuck her fingers in her ears. But she was still smiling, so it was okay.

"Well, I thought it was finally time for us to have . . . our . . . very . . . own . . ." She was speaking slowly to stretch out the suspense. Everyone squirmed in their chairs.

"Let it be a microscope, let it be a microscope," Hugo heard Gigi saying under her breath.

"Our very own class pet!" Mrs. Nukluk finished.

The whole class made a whoop of joy, even Boone. The Academy for Curious Squidges had never had a class pet before. Sometimes a mouse would wander into the classroom, then wander out again, but that was not the same thing.

"Is it a camel?" asked Malcolm. But a

camel in a cavern was too ridiculous, so no one even answered him.

Carefully, Mrs. Nukluk removed the top of the wooden crate. All the squidges leaned forward in their seats to try to see inside. Reaching into the crate, Mrs. Nukluk pulled out a large glass aquarium tank. She placed it on top of her desk. Inside the glass tank were wood chips, a wooden hut, some wooden bowls, and what looked like two hairy snowballs with long ears.

"*Ooooo!* What are they?" asked Pip.

"They are called Arctic Floofs," said Mrs. Nukluk.

"They look like guinea pigs, except with rabbit ears," said Boone.

Which was exactly what they looked like.

There were all kinds of questions after that, like:

What do we feed them? (Berries and leaves.)

Do they bite? (Only if you bite them first.)

Are the Floofs married? (That was Malcolm's question, and the answer was a deep breath from Mrs. Nukluk.)

Hugo had never had a pet before. He always thought it might be nice to have a pet bat. There were plenty of bats in Widdershins Cavern. He thought they were cute, with their little fox-faces, but he knew his mom would never let a bat live in his bedroom.

Hugo raised his hand.

"Can I hold one of the Floofs?" he asked.

And then, of course, the whole class wanted to hold them.

Mrs. Nukluk scooped one of the Floofs out of the tank. It made a funny little squeaking noise. Carefully, she put it in Hugo's hands. The Floof was warm, and its fur was silky soft. Hugo felt the Floof's heartbeat against the palm of his hand. With one finger he gently pet its little head, and the Floof made its squeaking sound again.

"He likes you," Gigi said.

Hugo sighed happily. An Arctic Floof was even better than a bat.

He sniffed its fur. "It smells like warm biscuits," he said.

After a moment, Mrs. Nukluk took the Floof from Hugo, much to Hugo's disappointment, and put it into Gigi's hands.

"We'll have to name them, of course," said Mrs. Nukluk.

"How about Cha Cha and Bumbles?" suggested Hugo.

"The names should rhyme," said Gigi. "How about Benny and Penny?"

"Or Mollie and Ollie?" said Pip.

"Or Lucus and Mucus," suggested Malcolm.

They argued over the names as the little Floof was passed around the class.

Finally, Mrs. Nukluk came to Boone. Boone cupped his hands together and held them out. Mrs. Nukluk put the Floof in them.

"Hello, little guy," he said to it softly. "Or girl."

Boone stared down at the Floof. It looked back up at him with its shiny black eyes.

Boone bent his head down and pressed his nose to the Floof's fur, sniffing in the warm biscuit smell.

"Mrs. Nukluk!!" shrieked Roderick. *"Stop him, Mrs. Nukluk! Boone is trying to eat the Floof!"*

"No, I'm not!" cried Boone.

"Yes, you were! You were just about to take a bite out of him!" insisted Roderick.

"I'm sure you're mistaken, Roderick," said Mrs. Nukluk.

"I'm sitting right next to him! I can see better than anybody. He opened his mouth like this." Roderick opened his mouth wide enough to fit a Floof in it.

The class gasped.

"I only wanted to sniff him," Boone said. He looked around the class at all the horrified faces. "Because he smells like biscuits . . ."

Okay, here's the part that I don't want to tell you. But I feel like I need to be perfectly honest. Hugo's face was horrified, too. Because even though Hugo didn't *really* think Boone would ever eat a Floof, he remembered what Roderick had said about Humans eating just about anything.

And though Hugo didn't *really* think that Boone had opened his mouth to take a bite out of the Floof, Boone *had* put his face awfully close to it . . .

Hugo looked at Boone. Boone looked back at Hugo, and he saw the shocked expression on his friend's face. Boone sighed. With the Floof still cupped in his hands, he stood up and walked to the front of the classroom. Very carefully, he handed the Floof back to Mrs. Nukluk.

"I think I'd better go home now," he said.

"Oh, Boone," said Mrs. Nukluk. "I'm sure we can work this out."

"Thanks anyway, Mrs. Nukluk." He put

out his hand. Mrs. Nukluk took it in her large hairy hand and shook it.

Then, after a sad little half-wave to Hugo, Boone headed out of the classroom. All the squidges turned around to watch him leave.

That's when two things happened:

1. Hugo's Monster Detector started to go *CLICK-CLICK-CLICK-CLICK!*

2. Everyone saw a grizzly green beast rush through the hallway outside the school.

10

The Adventures of Big Foot and Little Foot

I t's the Green Whistler!" cried Hugo.
The squidges screamed and jumped to their feet.

"Sit down, everyone!" ordered Mrs. Nukluk. "We'll all stay right here until that creature is caught."

"What will they do to it when they catch

it?" asked Boone, who was still standing near the door.

"I'm not sure, Boone," said Mrs. Nukluk. "Now come back in the classroom please."

But Boone shook his head. "Mrs. Nukluk, I am going to be a cryptozoologist," he said stoutly. "And that thing out there is a cryptid, so I have to help it if I can." Then he turned and dashed out the door.

It took Hugo a second to decide what he needed to do. Boone was his best friend. He had once saved Hugo from drowning in the Ripple Worm River. They were Big Foot and Little Foot, future cryptozoologists! If Boone was going after the Green Whistler, Hugo was, too.

He leapt out of his seat and ran out of the classroom. Behind him, he could hear Mrs. Nukluk yelling for him to come back. He knew he was going to be in big trouble. He kept going anyway.

"Wait for me, Boone!" he called when he spied Boone up ahead in a passageway. "I'm coming with you!"

Boone turned around, surprised to see Hugo.

"Are you sure?" Boone asked.

"I'm totally sure," Hugo replied.

Once again, I have to be honest with you. Hugo was not *totally* sure. He was only *mostly* sure. After all, they were chasing a dangerous monster. And on top of that, the monster might be a

squidge-eating monster, so you can't really blame Hugo for being a tiny bit not sure.

Hugo and Boone hurried along the passageway as quietly as possible. A few times, Boone's sneakers slapped against the floor, but Hugo's bare feet did not make a sound. Neither did the Monster Detector. That meant the Green Whistler was not nearby. Secretly, Hugo felt relieved.

The passageway widened, then narrowed, then twisted and turned. Hugo kept listening for the *click-click* of the Monster Detector or, even worse, the dreaded whistle of the Green Whistler. But the only sound he heard was the growling of his own stomach. It made him think of the acorn butter–and–raspberry cream sandwiches still sitting in his lunch bag back at school.

"Maybe the Green Whistler went a different way," Hugo said hopefully.

"Maybe," Boone said.

"Or it might have left the cavern altogether," Hugo said, his voice brightening.

But then they heard it:

Click-click-click.

Hugo looked down at his wrist. The weechie-weechie moths were flapping their wings. Hugo felt a lump of dread in the place where his acorn butter–and–raspberry cream sandwiches should have been.

"Does that mean what I think it means?" Boone asked.

Hugo nodded.

Boone smiled.

With a deep but whispery voice, Boone said, "In the dark, spooky cavern, Big Foot and Little Foot were hot on the trail of the legendary Green Whistler."

"What?" Hugo was confused.

In his regular voice, Boone said, "This

will be a chapter in
the book I'm going
to write about us one
day. You know . . . *The
Adventures of Big Foot
and Little Foot.*" He

glanced shyly at Hugo. "I mean . . . if you
still think that we make a good team and
all."

Hugo cleared his throat. In his deepest
voice, he whispered, "Big Foot and Little
Foot were so close to the monster they
could smell it."

They really could smell it, too. There
was a strange odor in the passageway—
both sharp and musty. It made their noses
wrinkle up.

Boone continued the story: "The cavern was swarming with poisonous snakes, hissing and slithering across their path." He looked over at Hugo, because this was sort of a lie.

"Nice touch," Hugo whispered approvingly.

Boone continued in his deep voice: "Still, they had to stop the beast before it hurt someone, or someone hurt it."

That was true, thought Hugo. Then he wondered out loud, "But how will we stop it?"

"I'm not sure yet," Boone said in his

regular Boone voice. "When the time comes, we'll know what to do." He said this with such confidence that Hugo felt certain Boone was right.

Hugo continued the story: "Even though there was danger all around them, Big Foot wasn't afraid, because Little Foot was with him. And Little Foot was the smartest, bravest, and best friend any squidge could ever have."

"Thanks, Hugo," Boone said quietly.

And that's when they knew everything would be okay between them.

11

Twists and Turns

Every so often the passageway split into two, and they had to figure out which way to go. They would try one passage, and if the Monster Detector stopped clicking, they would turn back and go the other way.

After a while, Boone asked, "Do you know where we are?"

Hugo looked all around him. Nothing was familiar.

"I'm not sure," Hugo answered.

The cavern was very large, and they had traveled through so many twists and turns that Hugo had lost track. Now Hugo remembered all the times he and Winnie were warned not to go wandering in the cavern. If they got lost, their mom and dad told them, it might be hours, or even days, before they were found again.

Or maybe never, a little voice in his head said. They'd be lost and alone with a squidge-eating monster on the loose!

Suddenly, Hugo stopped walking. He sniffed the air.

"Do you smell something?" Hugo asked.

"I can still smell the Green Whistler," Boone said.

"No," said Hugo, "something else."

Boone sniffed the air, then shook his head.

"I don't smell it," he said.

But Sasquatches are very good sniffers, much better than Humans. Hugo *did* smell something. It smelled like onions and the North Woods on a cool autumn day.

Up ahead, the passageway took a sharp turn to the right. As they approached the turn, the Monster Detector started *click-click-clicking* faster and faster. Just as Hugo and Boone rounded the bend, they saw something move in the distance.

There it was. The Green Whistler.

In the darkness, they could see the hulking shadowy figure lumbering along. Suddenly, the beast stopped and spun around. It was too dim to make out its face, but they could see the shine of its eyes.

"It sees us," Boone whispered.

Hugo nodded, but was too scared to whisper back.

The Green Whistler turned, and in a flash it disappeared through an open doorway just ahead of it.

Hugo sniffed the air again. The oniony, woodsy smell was even stronger.

Now Hugo knew what that smell was. It was a mushroom tart, just out of the oven. *And* he knew exactly where they were!

"Hurry, hurry!" Hugo cried. He took off running at top speed, with Boone close behind him. They ran down the passageway and through the open doorway . . . which just so happened to be the back door to the kitchen at the Everything-You-Need General Store and Bakery.

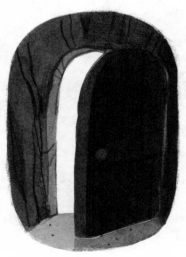

12

The Dreaded Whistle

The Green Whistler was standing with its back to them, looking at Hugo's grandpa. The monster's green fur was mangy and ratty. Hugo could hear its wheezing breath and could smell its sharp, stinging stench.

Grandpa was holding a steaming mushroom tart, staring back at the monster in shock.

"How? I don't . . . it's impossible . . ." Grandpa sputtered.

That's when the absolute worst thing happened.

The Green Whistler began to whistle.

The whistle was high-pitched, and it swooped up and down, almost like a song. Grandpa opened his mouth as though he was going to say something, but no words came out. Hugo's heart was thumping hard as he watched the Green Whistler move toward Grandpa. Any minute now, it was going to pounce.

"Do we know what to do yet?" Hugo said to Boone in a panicky voice.

"Yup," said Boone easily.

Boone walked right up to the monster.

Before Hugo could stop him, Boone threw his arms around it and hugged it. He hugged it so hard that the Green Whistler said, "Ow, Boone, you're squeezing! And for heaven's sake, what are you doing here?"

"What are *you* doing here, Grandma?" asked Boone.

Because that was who the Green Whistler was. Only you wouldn't have known it, because she was wrapped in the wooliest green blanket you'd ever seen.

"She's here to see me," said Grandpa, smiling fondly at Boone's grandma. "Now get some plates out of the cupboard, Hugo. Nothing goes better with a long explanation than a slice of mushroom tart."

13

Explanations

After Boone explained to his grandma about squidge school, he folded his arms and said to her, "Okay, your turn."

Boone's grandma swallowed her bite of mushroom tart and began: "When I was right about your age, Boone, and just as sassy—"

"And when I was a young squidge, a little older than Hugo," added Grandpa, "Ruthie and I ran into each other in the North Woods by accident."

"Do you know what he said to me when he first saw me?" Grandma Ruthie jerked a thumb toward Grandpa. "He said that I looked like a plucked turkey in a dress."

"Well, I'd never seen a Human before," said Grandpa.

"Anyway, I forgave him. Wasn't that big of me? And besides, I thought he looked like an overgrown gorilla. In the end, we became best friends."

"Like Boone and me," said Hugo.

"Exactly," said Grandpa. "We used to meet in secret, in a little room in the west

part of the cavern. I'd know she was there
because she would whistle for me."

Grandma Ruthie whistled the same tune she had whistled a few minutes before.

"I recognized that whistle," Boone told Hugo. "That's when I knew the Green Whistler was Grandma. She always whistles like that for me when I'm outside and she wants me to come in for dinner."

"Yes, and you always pretend you don't hear," she said to Boone, reaching out and giving his ear a tweak.

"Ruthie would bring a picnic lunch and a blanket," continued Grandpa, "and

we would sit in our secret room and talk and laugh and play games for hours. She taught me how to play poker."

"I always won," Grandma Ruthie said.

Grandpa leaned over to Hugo and Boone and said quietly, "I think she cheated."

"Oh, I did!" Grandma Ruthie said, laughing.

"We had the best time, didn't we?" Grandpa said to her.

"The best," she agreed. Then her face grew serious. "Until one day . . ."

"Oh yes," Grandpa's face grew serious, too.

"One day, I was waiting in the room with my picnic lunch and my blanket, whis-tling for your Grandpa. I was hungry, so between whistles, I nibbled on some fried chicken—"

"Disgusting stuff!" Grandpa said.

"Well, I always brought jelly sandwiches for you, didn't I? Anyway, right then a Sasquatch was walking outside, and he heard me whistling. I spotted him just in time. Right before he peeped into the

room, I threw the blanket over my head— yes, it was that very same green blanket. Well, that Sasquatch took one look at me under the green blanket, and then he saw the chicken bones on the ground, and he took off running."

"That's how the story of the Green Whistler got started," said Grandpa.

"Soon after that, my family moved to the city. We packed up and left, and I never even had a chance to say good-bye to my friend."

"Ah, so that's what happened," Grandpa said. "I had always wondered."

"Is that why we moved to the North Woods, Grandma?" Boone asked. "So you could find Hugo's grandfather?"

"Don't be silly," Grandma Ruthie said. "We moved here for the peace and quiet, and because a childhood in the woods is the best sort of childhood of all." Then she smiled at Hugo's grandfather. "*And* we moved here so that I could find my dear old friend again . . . and beat him in a few rounds of poker."

14

The Green Blanket

It was then that Hugo realized something.

"I guess my Monster Detector never really worked after all, since you're not a monster," he said to Grandma Ruthie.

"I should say not," she replied.

Hugo undid the strap and tossed the Monster Detector on the table in disgust.

"I collected all those Monster Card wrappers for nothing."

Grandma Ruthie picked up the Monster Detector and examined it with great interest.

"What are those little white specks behind the glass?" she asked.

"They're called weechie-weechie moths," said Hugo. "They were clicking like crazy the whole time we were following you."

"*Ahhh!*" Grandma Ruthie said as though she understood something now. Taking the Monster Detector, she went over to her green blanket, which she had left on a stool in the corner.

Click-click, went the Monster Detector.

CLICK-CLICK-CLICK!!! CLICK-CLICK-CLICK!!!

"See!" said Hugo. "It doesn't work. The blanket isn't a monster."

"Maybe not to you, but it is to the weechie-weechie moths," Grandma Ruthie said. "Haven't you noticed the smell?" She picked up the mangy-looking blanket and brought it over to them.

Hugo, Boone, and Grandpa all wrinkled their noses at the sharp, musty stench.

"We thought that was the smell of the Green Whistler," said Boone.

"It's the smell of mothballs!" said Grandma Ruthie. "I stored the blanket with them. Moths hate the smell of mothballs!"

The weechie-weechie moths were flapping their wings so frantically that Hugo took the Monster Detector from Grandma Ruthie, just to rescue them. He put the Monster Detector back on his wrist. He'd grown sort of fond of the weechie-weechie moths. They might even make pretty good pets, he thought.

"Ruthie, why on earth were you running around with that nasty blanket over you anyway?" asked Grandpa.

"I always wear it when I come to the cavern," she said.

"You mean you've been here before?"

"Many times. I waited in our secret room, but you never showed up. So I figured I'd snoop around the cavern. I knew the other Sasquatches would run away from me if I was dressed like the Green Whistler. Sasquatches are such scaredy-cats!"

"Not Hugo," Boone said. "He's brave."

"Well, maybe not *totally* brave," Hugo confessed. "I think I'm just *mostly* brave."

"So . . ." Grandma Ruthie turned to Grandpa. "Do you think a plucked turkey and an overgrown gorilla can still be friends?"

"I'm certain of it," Grandpa said.

15

Floating Post Office

When Hugo got back home that day he went straight to his room.

There was a little stream that ran right into Hugo's bedroom through a hole in the bottom of the wall. It wiggled across the room and then went out another hole in the wall by Hugo's toy chest. In a funny way, that little stream was Hugo and Boone's personal floating post office, since that's how they sent messages to each other.

Opening up his toy chest, Hugo pulled out a little wooden boat. He had carved it himself, and it could float as well as a boat twenty times its size. This is the note that Hugo wrote to Boone:

HI, BOONE.

WHEN I WENT BACK TO CLASS TODAY, MRS. NUKLUK WAS PRETTY MAD AT ME FOR LEAVING. BUT WHEN I TOLD HER ABOUT WHAT HAPPENED, SHE SAID IF I WROTE IT ALL OUT IN MY BEST HANDWRITING, IT WOULD COUNT FOR THE ENGLISH CLASS THAT I MISSED. I EVEN INCLUDED THE PART ABOUT THE POISONOUS SNAKES. HA-HA!

ALSO, GUESS WHAT? THE SQUIDGES WANT YOU TO COME BACK TO OUR SCHOOL! THEY SAID ANYONE WHO WOULD RUN OFF TO HELP A MONSTER WOULD NEVER EAT A FLOOF (WELL, RODERICK WASN'T CONVINCED, BUT TOO BAD FOR HIM). SO PLEASE COME BACK TO SCHOOL, BOONE. THINK OF ALL THE ADVENTURES WE COULD HAVE IF WE SAW EACH OTHER EVERY DAY!

YOUR FRIEND ALWAYS,

HUGO

Hugo rolled up the note and put it in a little glass bottle with a stopper. He put the bottle in the toy boat and carefully placed the boat on the stream. Then he took a deep breath and blew it out on the little boat's stern. The boat wobbled at first before it floated down the stream, through the little hole in the wall, and out into the Big Wide World.

16

Blueberry Ink

The next day, however, Boone was not at school.

Hugo was crestfallen. Even though Boone had only been at the Academy for Curious Squidges for one day, the classroom just wasn't the same without him. The empty seat beside Roderick seemed like it was waiting for

Boone to sit in it. Even helping to name the Floofs didn't cheer Hugo up. (The class finally settled on the names Daisy and Mr. Biggles.)

Art class was first. They were learning how to make ink out of blueberries. It was something Hugo had been looking forward to doing for weeks, but he just couldn't feel happy about anything today.

Mrs. Nukluk gave everyone a wooden bowl full of blueberries and a wooden pestle. The first thing they had to do was smash all the berries to get the juice out of them. The squidges smashed and bashed so loudly that no one heard the footsteps running down the hall outside the school and into the classroom.

"Sorry I'm late!" a voice cried from the back of the room.

Everyone turned around and there was Boone, with his thirty-eight freckles and his brown paper bag.

"You're here!" cried Hugo.

"Of course. I would have come sooner, but I just got your note a few minutes ago," said Boone. "The river's current is running a little slow."

Which, by the way, is one of the drawbacks of a floating post office.

"Mrs. Nukluk," said Boone, "if it's okay with you, I'd like to go to squidge school. I don't know a lot about snuds and stuff like that, but I'm a quick learner."

"Boone, we would be *honored* to have you in our class," said Mrs. Nukluk.

The whole class cheered. Well, everyone except Roderick, but he didn't yell "Boo!" or anything like that either. Some squidges (and people, too) just take a little longer to change their minds about things.

Right then Hugo had an idea. He raised his hand, then waved it around to show that he had something extra important to say.

"Yes, Hugo?"

"I have an idea," Hugo said.

"What is it?" Mrs. Nukluk asked.

"I don't want to say it out loud."

Mrs. Nukluk considered. "You can come up here and whisper it to me."

Hugo walked up to Mrs. Nukluk's desk. He leaned close to her ear. He had never

been that close to Mrs. Nukluk's head before. It smelled like bananas.

Hugo cupped his hand around his mouth and whispered his idea into Mrs. Nukluk's ear. Then he leaned away so he could see her face. It looked happy.

"That's an *excellent* idea, Hugo," she said.

"Thanks," Hugo said. "Can I whisper something else?"

"All right."

Hugo cupped his hand and leaned close. He didn't really have anything else to say. He just wanted to smell her head again. But since he had to say *something*, he asked, "Why does your head smell like bananas?"

Mrs. Nukluk looked at him. He looked back at her. Then she leaned over and whispered in his ear, "Banana shampoo."

Hugo nodded. "Got it," he said.

Mrs. Nukluk liked Hugo's idea so much that she went right to the art closet and gathered up all the supplies. Then, without telling the class why, she led everyone out of the classroom and into the hallway just outside the school's entrance.

Hugo climbed onto Mrs. Nukluk's shoulders. Mrs. Nukluk climbed on a chair. She handed Hugo a container of blueberry ink and a pine-needle paintbrush. In his best, most careful handwriting, Hugo added two new words to the school sign:

ACKNOWLEDGMENTS

Sasquatches know that we all need help if we want to do things right, and that's why I want to thank my wonderful "Sasquatch Community." Major thanks to my editor, Erica Finkel, for her clear-sighted wisdom. I am forever grateful to my agent, Alice Tasman, who is even better than thirty jars of acorn butter. Thanks to Felicita Sala for bringing Hugo and his friends to life with her beautiful illustrations. Big thanks to my publicist, Kimberley Moran, and the entire Abrams team for spreading the word about Hugo and Boone. And finally, as always, thanks to my practically perfect husband, Adam, and my own squidge, Ian.